The Smart Princess

Princess

And Other Deaf Tales

The Smart Princess

And Other Deaf Tales

A Project of the Canadian Cultural Society of the Deaf

By
Keelin Carey
Kristina Guévremont
Nicole Marsh
Nicholas Meloche-Kales
Déna Ruiter-Koopmans

Illustrated by
Kelly C. Halligan
Eugeniu Televco
Colleen C. Turner

Second Story Press

Library and Archives Canada Cataloguing in Publication

The smart princess.

Written and illustrated by winners of the Ladder Awards.
ISBN 1-896764-90-8
ISBN 978-1-896764-90-0

1. Deaf—Juvenile fiction. 2. Children's stories, Canadian (English)
3. Deaf, Writings of the, Canadian (English) 4. Canadian fiction—
21st century.

PS8323.D35S53 2006   jC813'.010835272   C2006-901349-7

Copyedited by Alison Reid
Front cover illustration by Colleen Turner

Printed and bound in Canada

*Second Story Press gratefully acknowledges the support of the
Ontario Arts Council and the Canada Council for the Arts for our
publishing program. We acknowledge the financial support of the
Government of Canada through the Canada Book Fund.*

Published by
Second Story Press
20 Maud Street, Suite 401
Toronto, Ontario, Canada
www.secondstorypress.ca

These stories by Deaf youth and young adults from the Deaf community are a product of the Ladder Awards II: Story Swap™ Program graciously funded by Human Resources and Social Development Canada, National Literacy Secretariat (NLS). We wish to honor the memories of two beloved individuals with these stories — Clayton Valli, American renowned American Sign Language poet who mentored many Deaf Canadians, and Phoebe Gilman, Canadian award-winning picture book author and illustrator who mentored many Deaf Canadians in the first Ladder Awards Project.

Joanne Cripps and Anita Small, MSc, EdD
Co-Directors
Deaf Culture Centre
Canadian Cultural Society of the Deaf

Contents

Illustrator: Colleen C. Turner

by Déna Ruiter-Koopmans

Once upon a time a little girl was born to a king and queen. They named her Lyla. Everyone agreed that Princess Lyla was adorable indeed.

When their daughter was a few months old, the king and queen noticed that she couldn't hear anything. They clapped their hands and called her name, but Lyla didn't respond. She just kept playing quietly as if she hadn't heard them at all.

They decided to take her to the doctor, whose name was Sarah Jane. She gave Lyla many tests, and soon found that the girl was Deaf. Because Dr. Sarah Jane did not know much about Deaf people, she told the king and queen not to bother trying to teach their daughter anything. Deaf people, she was sure, could not learn.

Luckily, the king and queen had already noticed that their daughter was, in fact, very smart. So they ignored the doctor's advice, and when Lyla was old enough, they enrolled her in the Royal School for Deaf Girls, a few hours away by royal coach.

Although it meant that their daughter had to spend

time away from them, the king and queen were happy that she would now be learning many things, just like other children. But Lyla was scared. When she got to the school, she saw that everyone used sign language, which she didn't understand. And she missed her parents. It was all very strange for the princess, and so at first she didn't like the school.

But by the second week she began to understand the signs the people were making with their hands. She was learning new things all the time. And best of all, she started to make friends with kids who were Deaf just like herself.

From then on, Lyla spent part of every year at home with her parents and part of the year at the Royal School for Deaf Girls. The king and queen learned to sign and so did everyone else in the palace, and all the royal relatives throughout the kingdom. Well, almost everyone — everyone except Lyla's snooty Aunt Belle. Lyla didn't mind about Aunt Belle because mostly her life was very good, full of friends and people who knew how smart she was and thought she was terrific.

One day when Lyla came home to the palace for a visit, she found that her parents had been called away to a far corner of the kingdom. They had left instructions that Lyla was to stay with her Aunt Belle, who lived out in the country.

Now, the king and queen knew that Aunt Belle had never learned to sign. "She's so snooty!" they said to each other. "Too snooty to learn anything new!" But she was family, they agreed, and Lyla would be safe with her.

What they didn't know was that Aunt Belle thought that because Lyla was Deaf, she wasn't smart. She thought that Deaf people couldn't read, write, sew or do any of the million things that people learn to do. And she thought that talking in sign looked ridiculous (mostly because she couldn't understand it).

When Lyla arrived at snooty Aunt Belle's home, her aunt sat her down and said, "Lyla, I am going to teach you how to speak."

What is she saying? thought the princess. Although she couldn't understand what snooty Aunt Belle was telling her, she could see that something was wrong. What could it be? Finally, her aunt pointed at Lyla's mouth. *Does she think I'm hungry?* Lyla wondered. She shook her head no and smiled. Aunt Belle frowned and pointed again at Lyla's mouth. *Does she think I'm having trouble breathing?* Lyla smiled again to show she was okay. Aunt Belle scowled as she pointed a third time at Lyla's mouth, and all at once the princess understood.

"No, no, no," she signed frantically, as her eyes filled

with tears. "I don't want to learn how to talk! I can sign! I am fine just as I am, and I am proud to be Deaf."

"This is nonsense!" shouted Aunt Belle. "You will do as I tell you, you will learn to speak, and you will, above all, stay put!"

Now, as we know, Lyla was a smart girl. She knew that signing wasn't nonsense, she knew that speaking was not for her, and she knew that, if she stayed put, as snooty Aunt Belle seemed to want, she would be miserable. So later that night, when everyone else was asleep, the princess made her escape. She knew what kinds of things make sounds that people could hear, so she walked very, very quietly, past Aunt Belle's bedroom, past the guards in the hall, past the watchman at the front door, and out into the still, dark night.

Lyla was determined to get herself back home. She made her way to the road, and waited for a passing carriage that might give a princess a ride. She waited and waited and waited. No carriage came. But after a long while, a truck appeared out of the night, slowing down and then stopping just up the road from where Lyla was waiting. As the driver climbed out to stretch his legs, Lyla crept up to the back of the truck and got ready to climb in with whatever was in there. And what, she wondered as she lifted up the tarp, might that be?

Her nose told her before eyes did. The truck was loaded with pigs! Big, fat, huge, smelly pigs.

But Lyla was a smart girl, and she knew this was no time to act like a princess. She quickly climbed up into the back and squeezed in between two fat pigs. Just as the truck started up again, another pig snorted and walked across her dress, leaving muddy prints.

This was pretty bad! She couldn't wait until they got nearer the palace so she could get out of this. But she was determined to stay in the truck — smelly, muddy pigs and all — because each turn of the truck's big wheels took her farther away from snooty Aunt Belle, who thought Deaf people couldn't learn, and closer to her home, where everyone signed, and everyone knew how smart she was.

Peeking out from under the tarp, the princess soon began to recognize familiar landmarks. They were getting near her home! As soon as the driver stopped again, she jumped out, but not before signing goodbye to the pigs. After all, it wasn't their fault that they stank so badly.

Lyla soon caught sight of the royal palace, and all the discomfort of her journey was forgotten. She ran as fast as she could to the door. When the queen saw Lyla, her face lit up. "My dear daughter is home," she signed.

The queen herself had arrived home only the day before. She knew nothing about how snooty Aunt Belle had been to her daughter. When the princess told her mother what had happened, the queen was horrified. She shook her head, thought for a few minutes, and then folded her arms. "She will have to go to school," she announced.

"Snoo — I mean, Aunt Belle will have to go to *school*?" Lyla asked.

"Yes. She must go to the Royal School for Adults, to learn that smart people come in all shapes and sizes. Some smart people write books, others build bridges. Some like pizza, some like pickles. Some smart people speak, and some smart people sign."

Years later when Lyla became the first Deaf queen, she made a law that all people had to learn to sign so that everyone could communicate better with her and with each other.

And do you know what became of snooty Aunt Belle? Once she finished school and learned to sign, Queen Lyla appointed her Royal Assistant to the Queen and Head of the Royal School for Adults for the whole kingdom. And she was no longer snooty at all.

by Nicholas Meloche-Kales

In the year 2012, on a beautiful April morning, two groups of astronauts met for the first time in the minutes leading up to the launch of a space shuttle. Together, these six people would make up the crew for the shuttle's mission, a mission that would take them far into outer space. Members of one group — Kristy, Nicray, and Tara — were signing to each other as they prepared for the launch. The other group — Joe, Joshua, and Jessica — shouted to each other over the ferocious roar of the shuttle as it prepared it for its mission in far distant corners of the universe.

When all the systems were ready, Joe shouted out at the top of his lungs, "Let's launch!"

"What did you say?" Kristy asked. "I can't read your lips because the shuttle is shaking so much."

Joe didn't notice Kristy's question, but Jessica did. "We're launching," she signed to Kristy, and then shouted out the words so that Joe and Joshua would hear over the rocket's roar. Then Jessica pushed the big red button to fire the launch rockets. Tara pushed the big blue button to fire the auxiliary engines, and

Illustrator: Eugeniu Televco

zoom! The shuttle shot up into the sky, faster and faster, speeding away from Earth.

"We are in space!" Nicray began to sign, and this time Joe noticed.

"What the heck are you using your hands for?" he asked Nicray.

"Three of us are Deaf," Kristy reminded her colleague. "But if we all sign and speak, the whole crew can communicate."

Joshua was confused. "Don't all of you have cochlear implants? I thought all Deaf people used them, so that nowadays everyone can hear."

Nicray signed, "I don't like to use the cochlear implant because it doesn't always work and because it doesn't feel like it would be me. Lots of people don't use them."

Kristy translated Nicray's signs for Joshua, but Joshua was still confused. "How did you know what I said, if you can't hear my voice and I didn't sign?"

Nicray replied, "I can lip-read."

Joshua thought about this, and turned to his hearing colleagues. "So if they can read our lips, and they can speak, then I guess we can converse with them. And when they speak, we can understand them. But most of the time, they sign. And when they sign, we can't understand what they're saying to us."

"I can," said Jessica. "I've known how to sign since I was a kid. I thought you guys did too."

"No," said Joshua. "I wish I did."

Joe looked skeptical, but didn't say a word. In a few minutes, all of them had stopped talking, because what was going on outside the shuttle had grabbed everyone's attention.

Past the moon's orbit they flew. "Cool," signed Kristy, Nicray, and Tara. "Cool," said Joe, Joshua, and Jessica.

A short time later, Mars came into view. "Wow," signed Kristy, Nicray, and Tara. "Wow," said Joe, Joshua, and Jessica.

Jupiter appeared. "Amazing," signed Kristy, Nicray, and Tara. "Amazing," said Joe, Joshua, and Jessica.

On and on through space, the shuttle sped past stars, past planets, farther and farther from Earth, on and on toward the vast unknown.

Suddenly Jessica gasped. "Look at the black hole!" She signed and then spoke.

"It looks dangerous," said Joe.

Jessica wasn't so sure. She signed and then spoke again: "We've got to go through the hole to see a different solar system," she reminded them.

"No way," said Joe. "I think we should switch directions and get away from it."

Before the crew could agree on a course of action, the decision was made for them: the force of the black hole's gravity began to pull the shuttle in. No matter how hard the six astronauts struggled to regain control of the spacecraft, they were powerless against the pull of the black hole.

Deeper and deeper it went, into space that got blacker and blacker. But at last Tara said, with her hands and then her voice, "I see some light! One star with three planets." All six astronauts were excited and relieved — light might mean a place where they could land!

Kristy warned them: "We can't stop there if there is no oxygen."

"One of those three planets looks exactly like Earth. It has oxygen!" Tara shouted and then signed. "Let's try that one. We'll feel right at home. In fact, we can call it 'Earth 2!' "

In no time they identified a spot where they could land. Carefully they brought the shuttle down to the surface of Earth 2 and prepared to leave the ship. Just before they opened the door, Joe confessed to his colleagues, "I'm really afraid." Joe was now more careful about letting everyone see his lips when he spoke, using his eyes and face more, and adding some hand movements. When he told them about his fear, all the other astronauts nodded their heads in agreement.

They were all afraid.

But they pushed aside their fears, opened the shuttle door, and climbed out of the ship. Slowly they looked around, and soon they began to smile. Jessica said and then signed what they were all thinking: "All the people look … like people! They're just like us." Joshua began to relax a little, grinning with excitement and relief.

Soon the astronauts noticed something else.

"They're all signing to each other!" yelled Joe.

It was true. All the people on Earth 2 were communicating with their hands only. There were no voices.

One of the Earth 2 people signed to Joshua. "Who are you?" Joshua listened as Kristy interpreted, and then he replied.

"I am from Earth and my name is Joshua." Kristy signed his response.

"My name is Matt," signed the Earth 2 person.

"Wow! All the people around here can communicate with hands," signed Tara.

Matt answered, "We use American Sign Language."

"That's awesome," Nicray signed. "We use it too!"

Kristy, Nicray, and Tara were thrilled to find this new planet so compatible. But Joshua and Joe felt differently.

"I want to go back to Earth!" said Joshua.

"Yeah. Let's go," said Joe.

Tara stopped them as they raced back to the shuttle. "You can't!" she told them. "The black hole pulled us here. We don't have any fuel strong enough to overcome the gravitational force of the black hole. We can't get back."

"Oh, no!" Joe cried. "You mean we're going to be stuck here with all these DEAF people?!"

For a moment everyone was quiet, staring at Joe. "Yes," said Kristy, "with Deaf people. Just like Tara, Nicray, and me. Here on Earth 2, it seems that hearing people have special needs."

"What do you mean?!" Joshua exclaimed. "I don't have special needs! I can hear better than anyone on this planet."

Tara shrugged. "But you and Joe don't know the language that's spoken here. That means that you and Joe have different needs."

"Now you know how I feel on Earth," said Nicray. "That's why I'd rather stay here."

The three Deaf astronauts were very excited. Earth 2 had billions of Deaf people just like them. There were some hearing people too, but they had all learned to sign. And everyone seemed to be very happy.

"It may be hard for a while," Kristy said, "but it's only till Earth can send a bigger rocket to rescue us. In the meantime, we'll teach you to sign. Jessica can help, since she already knows how. We're all in this together, and we can all stay friends."

Joe and Joshua looked at each other, and at Jessica, and their Deaf crewmates. They grinned. "When can we start sign school?"

by Nicole Marsh

Sometimes

Sometimes it's hard for Deaf and hearing people to learn and live together. Deaf people can have difficulty in a hearing school. I know this from first-hand experience because I used to go to a hearing school. I felt very isolated from everyone else because they wouldn't or couldn't talk to me. The hearing students in my class were sometimes very cruel and teased me. I remember one recess, I was at my desk reading a book while other kids were talking to each other. Suddenly they all started to laugh. One girl went up to the chalkboard and wrote, "Mr. Smith* sucks, by Nicole." I didn't want my teacher to think I had done it, so I went up to erase the writing. Two of the girls took chalkboard erasers and made a mess on their own shirts. My teacher came in, saw the mess on the girls' shirts, saw the chalkboard eraser in my hand and got mad at me. I went to the principal's office and they called my mom. She knew I wouldn't do anything like that. When the true story came out, the other girls got in trouble and hated me even more than they had before.

Illustrator: Kelly C. Halligan

Then I switched schools. My whole family moved to St. John's so I could go to the Newfoundland School for the Deaf. When I started there, I didn't know any signs at all. I felt a bit like a fish out of water. But the students were very different. Lots of people were really nice to me. No one teased me any more or played tricks on me.

Eventually I relaxed and started taking everything in. The best time ever was when I met Renee. She is a great signer, and I couldn't sign at all. It didn't matter. Her patience and my curiosity broke all the barriers. We became friends, and I owe my ability to sign mostly to her.

Without this new school, I wouldn't be able to be myself. I'd still be the shy girl who sits alone in the corner, reading. It's sad to say, but I think hearing and Deaf people can't always learn together. Some hearing people are too prejudiced to see who we are.

*Name changed

Illustrator: Kelly C. Halligan

My
Tiger

by Keelin Carey

Under the twinkling stars of a midnight-deep sky, a house was settling down to sleep. One light shone out from an upstairs window. Through the glass could be seen a pink bedroom, with stuffed toys and dolls in every nook and cranny. In the middle of the room stood a pink bed, where a little girl lay snuggled beneath the covers, signing to the stuffed tiger that she cuddled close beside her. As she signed, she imagined that he understood her. He looked as though he did! But she knew better.

Soon her arms grew heavy, and her eyes began to close. Just before she drifted off, she reached over to her Tiger, rubbed his belly, and signed to him the same wish she wished every night. "I wish you would come to life. You could visit me, play with me, and help me whenever I need you. But I know it can't happen." And with a sigh, she closed her eyes, and went to sleep.

But on this night, under the twinkling stars of a midnight-deep sky, something happened. On this night, the little girl's wish found its way into Tiger's heart, and went deep inside of it.

His heart began to beat.

His eyes began to glitter with hot green fire. His fuzzy nose became smooth and quivering, alert to the scents in the room. His stubby little tail grew long and powerful, and began to twitch and swirl, until finally he brought it down on the pillow with a THUMP!

The little girl's eyes flew open. Her wish had come true! Tiger was real.

In an instant, the girl found herself sitting on cool green grass as a hot sun rose above the hills, shining red-orange-pink among the trees. Delicious smells tickled her nose: orchids and lilacs, dewdrops and salty sea air. Her eyes drank in huge, colorful flowers, tall grasses, and rainbow parrots that darted among palm trees loaded with coconuts.

But a moment later, dark clouds began to block the sun. Behind her, something — or someone — was quietly moving closer. Bushes rustled. Twigs snapped. Something was creeping up on her.

Out sprang an ugly face — beady eyes, hairy ears, and an ugly wicked smile. The dreadful figure loomed over the girl, and brought his horrible face up close to hers.

The little girl screamed, and all around her, the jungle screamed too: parrots flapped their wings, monkeys bounced up and down. A gust of wind carried the girl's screams as they slashed the air. The monstrous face jumped back in fear, covering its hairy ears with its horrible hands.

And when he showed his fear, a strange and wonderful change occurred. The monster melted away, and a different creature stood in his place. The ugly and wicked face gave way to the face of a jungle cat, a face that the little girl knew and loved. "My Tiger!" she signed. "My friend!"

Relief flooded her body, and she threw her arms around her Tiger. He licked her face and began to purr so powerfully that the ground beneath them trembled. She tossed him his favorite ball, the green one that sparkled like his eyes, and they played for hours, all through the magical night with the red-orange-pink sun.

When the little girl awoke back in her bed, she found her faithful stuffed Tiger beside her as usual, with his plastic eyes, his fuzzy nose, and his stumpy little tail. But now she knew that he *could* come to life, through her imagination. He could visit her in her dreams, play with her, and help her when she needed him.

"Good morning," she signed to her nighttime companion — her Tiger, her friend.

Illustrator: Colleen C. Turner

Best Friends

by Kristina Guévremont

Ernie was feeling very lonely as he went for a walk along the creek. He wanted a best friend but no one liked him because he was so, so big. Morty was walking on the other side of the creek. He was lonely as well. Morty didn't have any friends because he was so, so small.

When they were closer, Ernie stopped and looked at Morty on the other side of the creek. Morty decided to give a friendly wave, hoping he'd make a new friend. Ernie waved back. They were both so happy that someone finally wanted to know them.

Morty tried to introduce himself, but Ernie looked puzzled.

"I'm sorry. I can't see your signing — you're too far away," Ernie signed. Morty walked around in search of a vine, and when he found one close to the creek, he swung across, and landed at Ernie's feet.

Morty looked way, way up at Ernie, and started to sign again. Ernie looked way, way down at Morty; he was still puzzled. Morty tried to sign bigger, but Ernie was baffled. Even bigger — still baffled. However hard Morty tried, his signing was so small that Ernie couldn't understand him.

"I have an idea," signed Ernie. "We could go and see Mikula the Wise. She can solve any problem. Maybe she can figure out a way for us to understand each other's signing." Morty had heard of Mikula the Wise. Everyone had heard of Mikula the Wise! And Morty agreed — if anyone could solve a problem like theirs, she could. At first Ernie couldn't tell that Morty was signing his agreement, but eventually he understood. And so the two new friends started on their journey, unable to communicate very well, but happy to be together, and hopeful that soon they would be able to chat just as all friends do.

The journey before them was long, and they could not pass the time in conversation. They were so frustrated — each of them had found a friend, but without communication, each one was lonely still.

As they made their way through a village, they passed by a store, and Morty got an idea. While Ernie waited, Morty went in bought a note pad and a pen. Now they could communicate as they traveled on their way to Mikula the Wise. "Great idea," wrote Ernie.

The thoughts and comments of the two companions flew back and forth between them, as Morty scribbled out questions and ideas in his tiny handwriting, and Ernie carefully wrote out his replies. It took a lot more time than signing, but they had time to spare, as they traveled on in search of Mikula the Wise.

Each one told the other about his life. They'd had quite different experiences, with one being so, so big, and the other being so, so small. Ernie described one bad experience he'd had with being big: "I had a best friend who was an aardvark. His name was Andy and he was hearing. We aren't best friends anymore."

"Why?" Morty wrote.

"Once he took me to see his favorite anthill, the place where he got all of his juiciest, crunchiest food. All of a sudden he started to scream and cry. 'What's the matter?' I signed. I was mystified. He signed in anger, 'You are worthless, stupid, blind, and fat! I never want to see you again!' and walked away. And we never did see each other again."

"Oh! That's a very mean insult," said Morty. "Why did he call you that?"

"It turns out that I had accidentally stepped on his favorite anthill."

"Oh, no!" Morty wrote. "That must have been embarrassing for you! I always thought it would be so much easier to be big, but now I'm not so sure."

The two continued on their way, passing the note

pad and pen back and forth, sharing their stories, until, far in the distance, they saw a shimmering golden palace, shaped like a lion's head: the palace of Mikula the Wise! Morty raised his arms in excitement and started jumping up and down. Ernie started jumping too, with jumps so powerful that the trees started to shake. Leaves fluttered down all around them. "Hey!" signed the trees, blaming Ernie for their dropping leaves.

"Sorry," Ernie apologized, and he and Morty hurried on their way, to seek the help of Mikula the Wise.

Half an hour later, they finally arrived at the shimmering golden palace that was shaped like a lion's head. They walked nervously up the stairs to the huge door, knocked, and waited. After a moment, the door opened. There stood Mikula the Wise.

"Please come in," she signed, and the two travelers stepped into the palace. "Follow me," said Mikula, as she opened a door marked "The Solutions Room."

Ernie and Morty followed her in. When they got inside, Ernie's big, big jaw dropped open, and Morty's tiny little eyes opened wide. They looked around in amazement. The walls were covered in magnificent gold and pink drapes, but there was no furniture anywhere in the room — just three cushions, one big and two small, on the wooden floor. Mikula led Ernie to the big cushion. He sat down and stretched out his big legs right to the edge of the cushion. Then she led Morty to a small cushion. Morty was so small, he covered only an inch of his cushion, and almost disappeared into the middle of it.

Mikula the Wise smiled a little smile, sat down on the third cushion, and gracefully signed, "What may I help you with today?"

Morty explained the problem. "Ernie and I just met this morning by the creek. We want to be friends, and we tried to sign to each other. But it's too hard — I'm too small and he's too big. When I sign, he can't see me. On the trip here, we have been writing to each other, but it takes too long. We would like to converse in the normal way."

Mikula the Wise sat quietly, deep in thought. She sat and sat, and thought and thought. Much time passed, and still she signed nothing. Morty and Ernie waited and waited, but after a time the weariness of their long journey got the better of them. Morty closed his eyes, and soon Ernie began to snore.

An hour later, Mikula tapped each of them with her finger. They both jumped.

"You startled me!" Morty signed, trying to catch his breath. Ernie blinked.

"I've found a solution to your problem," Mikula the

Wise signed. "Okay, Ernie, you stand here. Morty, you over there. Now Morty, climb up onto the tip of Ernie's trunk." Morty looked puzzled, but up he climbed.

"Now, Ernie," said Mikula, "lift your trunk until Morty is level with your eyes." Ernie followed Mikula's directions and lifted his trunk.

Mikula signed, "That's it. Now, Morty, sign something to Ernie with your cute little mouse hands." Morty started to sign ... and Ernie signed back! He had understood everything Morty had said. The two friends were so happy — finally they were able to talk to each other!

As Mikula led them out of the palace, they took turns, Morty with his little signing, and Ernie with his big signing, to say over and over again, "Thank you, thank you, thank you!"

Ernie and Morty lived together for a very long time. Morty spent most of his life on Ernie's trunk because all they did, all day long, was chat and chat and chat.

The Canadian Cultural Society of the Deaf and Second Story Press are pleased to bring you these lovely stories. Our thanks are extended to the many Deaf Canadians who participated in the Ladder Awards II: Story Swap™ Program and to the contributors — Keelin Carey, Kristina Guévremont, Nicole Marsh, Nicholas Meloche-Kales, Déna Ruiter-Koopmans, Kelly Halligan, Eugeniu Televco and Colleen Turner — who worked hard to expand Deaf experience in Canadian children's literature.

CCSD is a not-for-profit charitable organization founded in 1973. It represents over 450,000 Canadians and serves many more with its programs, cultural activities and Deaf heritage resources. CCSD preserves, encourages and advances the cultural interests of Canada's Deaf population with a focus on performing and visual arts, history, language, literature and heritage resources. In 2006, CCSD opened the Deaf

Culture Centre featuring a museum, art gallery, library, archives, multimedia production studio, board room, special event facilities, bookstore and gift shop. Contact us to see the other exciting resources we offer!

Joanne Cripps and Anita Small, MSc, EdD
Co-Directors
Deaf Culture Centre
Canadian Cultural Society of the Deaf
The Distillery Historic District
55 Mill Street, Building 5, Suite 101
Toronto, Ontario M5A 3C4
info@deafculturecentre.ca
http://www.ccsdeaf.com
416-548-8882 tty
416-548-8880 v